First American edition published in 2012 by Gecko Press USA,
an imprint of Gecko Press Ltd.

A catalog record for this book is available from the US Library of Congress.

Distributed in the United States and Canada by
Lerner Publishing Group, Inc.
241 First Avenue North
Minneapolis, MN 55401 USA
www.lernerbooks.com

This translation first published in New Zealand and Australia in 2007 by Gecko Press
PO Box 9335, Marion Square, Wellington 6141, New Zealand
Email: info@geckopress.com

Text and illustrations copyright © 2001 *l'école des loisirs*, Paris
Original title: *C'est moi le plus beau*

English translation copyright © Gecko Press 2007
All rights reserved. No part of this publication may be reproduced, transmitted or utilized in
any form, or by any means, electronic, mechanical, photocopying or otherwise, including
information storage and retrieval systems without the prior written permission of the
publisher.

Translator: Jean Anderson
Typesetting: Archetype, Wellington, New Zealand
Printing: Everbest, China

ISBN Hardback 978-1-877579-19-6

For more curiously good books, visit www.geckopress.com

Mario Ramos

I am so HANDSOME

Haverstraw King's Daughters
Public Library
10 W. Ramapo Rd.
Garnerville, NY 10923

GECKO PRESS

After a delicious breakfast, the incorrigible wolf put on his finest clothes.

"Ha! Ravishing! I'm off for a little stroll so everyone can admire me!" he said.

Before long, he came upon Little Red Riding Hood.

"Hmm, nice get-up! Tell me, my little wild strawberry, who's the handsomest around here?" asked the wolf.

"The handsomest? Why, that's you, Mister Wolf!" Red Riding Hood replied.

"There we have it!
Out of the mouths of babes, the truth.
I am the most elegant, the most
charming," bragged the wolf.

Just then, he met the three little pigs.

"Hey, little bacon bits! Still skipping about in the woods trying to lose weight? Tell me, little butterballs, who's the handsomest of all?" demanded the wolf.

"Oh, it's you! You're wonderful! You shine like a thousand stars!" the trembling piglets replied.

Haverstraw King's Daughters Public Library

"Heh, heh! I shine, I dazzle, I gleam and I glitter. I light up the woods with my presence. I am most marvelous," rejoiced the wolf.

Next, the wolf met the seven dwarves.

"Guys, that mine of yours is such a hole.
Why don't you take a break? You look dreadful.
Now, tell me, who's the handsomest of all?"

"The handsomest? Why, that's you, Big Wolf,"
chorused the little men.

"Ta-da! Tra-la-la! I'm the star of the woods,"
chanted the wolf. "Ha ha, I'm in
top form today. I certainly am!"

Soon he came across Snow White.

"Oh my word, so pale and peaky. Are you ill, poor girl? You must look after yourself. As I do. Take a good look at me and tell me, who's the handsomest of all?"

"Well…it must be you," replied the girl.

"Yeehaw! But of course, obviously!
Good answer, well done, child. I'm the king of the
woods. All eyes are on me. Thank you, thank you,
thank you, dear fans!" sang the wolf.

Finally, he met a baby dragon.

"Oh! Hello. What a surprise...
Is your mommy here?" asked the wolf,
looking all around.

"No, no. She's at home," replied the baby
dragon.

"Ah! Excellent, excellent!" said the wolf.
"Now tell me, you ridiculous little gizzard,
who's the handsomest of all?"

"The handsomest? It's my dad!
He taught me how to do this."

"But if you don't mind, no more stupid questions. We're in the middle of a game of hide and seek."